RUNED OMEGA

Laura Shenton

RUNED OMEGA

Laura Shenton

Iridescent Toad Publishing

Iridescent Toad Publishing.

Cover by Rosel Graphic Designs.

First edition. ISBN 978-1-913779-18-4

Chapter One

The suffocating heat in Pizza Time's kitchen had reached a point where Toni wondered if Hell itself might actually be cooler. The cramped space, barely large enough for two people to pass without awkwardly shuffling sideways, amplified every degree until the air felt heavy and oppressive. Beneath her polyester visor, her electric-blue hair – a defiant choice that had earned her more than a few disapproving looks during the hiring process – now hung in limp, sweaty strands against her neck. The ancient ventilation system wheezed pathetically overhead, offering little relief.

The industrial fryers hissed like angry cats, spattering oil onto her already-stained apron, while the conveyor belt ovens churned out an endless parade of mediocre pizzas. The pepperoni seemed to swim in pools of orange grease, and the cheese had that peculiar rubbery quality that came from being purchased in bulk from the lowest bidder. The smell, which had once made her mouth water during her first week, now clung to her clothes and skin like an unwanted embrace.

Greg, the manager, had mastered the art of looking busy while doing absolutely nothing. He perched in what he'd dubbed his "office" – really just a corner of the kitchen with a desk wedged between a stack of empty boxes and the mop sink. His wiry frame hunched over a desktop computer that belonged in a museum, its yellowed plastic case matching his nicotine-stained fingers as he pretended to scrutinise delivery invoices. The screen's glow illuminated his perpetual scowl, though Toni hadn't seen him actually complete any meaningful work in the three hours since her shift began.

The dinner rush had turned into a relentless assault of orders, each one accompanied by a customer who seemed personally offended by the concept of waiting. Toni juggled the phone, the counter, and the kitchen with the frantic energy of a circus performer, while

Greg remained firmly planted in his chair, occasionally offering unhelpful commentary about "picking up the pace".

"Where's my soda?" The demand cut through the cacophony of kitchen noise like a hammer through glass. The middle-aged man at the counter had that particular shade of facial redness that Toni had come to recognise as a warning sign – the same colour as her polyester uniform, which some sadistic corporate designer had chosen in a shade that could only be described as "aggressive ketchup".

"You didn't order one," she replied, her customer service voice strained to its breaking point. Her fingers gripped the edge of the counter, knuckles white with the effort of maintaining composure. The register tape from his order dangled accusingly between them, conspicuously lacking any mention of a beverage.

"I definitely did," he snapped, jowls quivering with indignation. A few drops of sweat trickled down his forehead, and Toni wondered if he was aware of how closely he resembled the pepperoni slices on the pizza he'd just ordered.

Swallowing both her pride and a particularly creative string of obscenities, Toni turned to the soda dispenser. The machine gurgled apologetically as she filled a cup with cola that had long since lost its enthusiasm for carbonation. She planted the drink in front of him with a smile so tight it made her jaw ache, mentally adding another tally to her "reasons to quit" list, which had grown longer than the ingredient list on their "special" sauce.

Behind her, a timer shrieked its warning about yet another pizza threatening to transform from merely disappointing to actively inedible. The phone started its shrill ring for what felt like the thousandth time that evening, and through the kitchen window, she could see a line beginning to form at the counter. A glance at the clock confirmed what her aching feet already knew – she still had four hours and twenty-three minutes left in her shift.

***

By the time the temperamental neon "Open Late" sign finally gave up its garish pink struggle against the darkness and blinked into merciful silence, the last customer had meandered out into the night, leaving behind greasy fingerprints on the glass door and a scattered collection of crumpled napkins. Toni attacked the counters with sanitising spray and a rag, each swipe more violent than the last, as if she could somehow scrub away the memory of the entire shift along with the dried tomato sauce and congealed cheese. The squeaking of the cloth against the laminate surface echoed her mounting frustration, punctuated by the occasional mutter under her breath. When she finally hurled the mop back into the supply closet, it clattered against the shelves with a satisfying crash that sent a cascade of paper towel rolls tumbling to the floor.

Greg materialised from his office cave just in time to witness her barely-contained fury, his thin lips twisted into what he probably thought was a sympathetic smile. "Rough night?" he asked, leaning against the door frame with all the casual indifference of someone who'd spent the evening safely ensconced behind a computer screen while chaos reigned beyond.

"No rougher than usual," Toni replied, her words sharp enough to slice through steel. She deliberately avoided eye contact as she yanked her backpack from her locker, the zipper protesting as she slung it over her shoulder with enough force to make the pins on the fabric rattle. "See you tomorrow." The words tasted bitter, like a promise she wished she didn't have to keep.

The city beyond Pizza Time's grimy windows pulsed with its usual nighttime energy, a stark contrast to the fluorescent-lit purgatory she'd just escaped. Streetlights cast pools of sickly orange illumination across the wet pavement, their ancient bulbs flickering in and out like dying fireflies. The ambient soundtrack of urban life filtered through the darkness – the distant thrum of bass from a nearby club, the persistent whisper of tires on wet asphalt, the occasional burst of laughter from late-night revellers who hadn't yet accepted that the party was over.

Her motorbike waited exactly where she'd left it, a sleek black shadow beneath one of the dimmer streetlights. The recent drizzle had left a constellation of water droplets across its frame, each one catching and fragmenting the artificial light into tiny starbursts. Under different circumstances, she might have found it beautiful. Tonight, it just looked tired.

Toni swung her leg over the seat, settling into the familiar leather with a sigh that carried the weight of her entire shift. She turned the key in the ignition, and kicked the starter with practiced motion – only to be rewarded with the sound of dying machinery. The engine coughed, sputtered, and fell silent with what seemed like deliberate spite.

"Not tonight," she muttered through clenched teeth, trying again with increasing desperation. Each attempt produced the same pathetic wheeze, followed by silence that seemed to mock her growing frustration. After the fifth try, she let her head fall forward against the handlebars, the cold metal pressing against her forehead as the reality of her situation sank in.

She knew the buses had stopped running over an hour ago. Her wallet, when she bothered to check it, contained a crumpled five-pound note and a collection of receipts – nowhere near enough for a taxi. The revelation settled in her stomach like lead; she had no choice but to walk the three miles home.

With a resigned sigh that seemed to start from somewhere around her toes, Toni began the long journey on foot. Each step reminded her of the hours she'd spent standing, and the polyester uniform – still redolent with the ghosts of a thousand pizzas – clung uncomfortably to her skin. The night air, despite its autumn chill, did nothing to disperse the persistent aroma of fryer oil and marinara sauce that had become her unwanted signature fragrance. As she walked, she tried to calculate how many more shifts it would take to afford the motorbike repairs she now knew were inevitable, but the maths only made her head hurt more than it already did.

Chapter Two

As Toni trudged along the deserted streets, her steel-toed boots scraping against the pavement with each weary step, an unusual sound pierced the urban quiet. It was a low, guttural whine – something between a wounded animal's cry and a sound that had no business existing in a civilised world. The noise raised the fine hairs on the back of her neck, still damp with sweat.

She halted mid-step, her body tensing as she turned towards the dark maw of an alleyway to her right. The narrow passage between buildings was thick with shadows, but something moved in the darkness – something substantial. A pair of eyes caught the meagre light and threw it back at her, burning with an unnatural brightness that seemed to pierce straight through her. As her vision adjusted to the gloom, the shape resolved itself into what appeared to be a dog, though its proportions were all wrong. It was massive, easily reaching her hip if it stood at full height, with shaggy black fur that hung in matted clumps around its muscular frame. The creature shifted its weight, and she noticed the way it favoured its right hind leg, keeping it lifted slightly off the ground.

"Hey there," Toni said, her voice barely above a whisper. She took a tentative step forward, the sound of her boot on concrete echoing off the brick walls. The smell of rotting cardboard and stale rain hung heavy in the air between them.

The animal's reaction was immediate – muscles bunching as it recoiled, lips peeling back to reveal teeth that seemed too large for any normal dog. Yet despite the threatening display, Toni noticed something in its posture that spoke more of fear than aggression. The creature's ears were pinned back not in anger but in distress, and its massive body seemed to curl in on itself, as if trying to appear smaller. There was something painfully vulnerable in its stance that resonated with her own exhausted state.

"Easy," she murmured, slowly lowering herself into a crouch. Her uniform trousers protested the movement, the polyester stretching tight across her knees. "I'm not gonna hurt you." The words came out gentle, the same tone she wished someone had used with her during tonight's shift.

The animal – and she was increasingly certain it wasn't just a dog but something closer to a wolf – fixed her with an intense stare. Its eyes were the colour of aged amber, and there was something in their depths that made her breath catch. Intelligence? Recognition? Whatever it was, it sent a shiver racing down her spine like ice water.

Moving with deliberate slowness, Toni reached into her backpack. Her fingers found the slightly squashed sandwich she'd meant to eat during her break, before the dinner rush had exploded into chaos. She tore off a chunk, the smell of peanut butter and jelly mixing incongruously with the alley's dank atmosphere.

The wolf watched her every movement with unnerving focus, its nose twitching slightly as she extended her hand with the offering. For a long moment, nothing moved except the steam rising from a nearby vent. Then, with a grace that seemed impossible for its size, the creature inched forward. Its movement was liquid shadow, each step precisely placed despite its injury. In a flash of movement almost too quick to follow, it snatched the food from her palm, sharp teeth barely grazing her skin as it wolfed down the morsel. Those amber eyes immediately locked back onto her face, an unmistakable expectation in their depths.

Toni found herself at a crossroads, weighing options in her tired mind. Stray dogs weren't uncommon in this part of the city – she'd seen plenty. But this was different. This creature radiated an aura of otherworldliness, its presence both magnetic and slightly terrifying. Every rational thought told her to walk away, to leave it to whatever fate had brought it to the alley. Yet something deeper, perhaps the same instinct that had always led her to root for the underdog, whispered that this creature needed her help. The way it held itself, the flash of intelligence in its eyes, the careful way it had taken food from her hand – all of it spoke of something more than just another abandoned animal.

"I guess you're coming with me," Toni announced, pushing herself back to her feet with a quiet groan. Her knees cracked in protest, reminding her of the hours she'd spent standing.

The wolf fell into step beside her as naturally as if they'd walked this route together a hundred times before. Despite its massive size, its paws made no sound against the concrete, moving with a silence that should have been impossible for such a large creature. The contrast between its ghostly quiet and her own tired footfalls was almost unsettling.

She couldn't help but think how surreal this all was. It wasn't like her to take risks, certainly not this kind. And yet here she was, leading a wolf – an actual wolf – back to her flat like it was the most normal thing in the world. The whole situation felt like something out of a bizarre dream. She had no idea what had possessed her to offer the animal shelter, but now that she was committed, she wasn't sure she could back out.

Maybe it was the loneliness that had settled into her life. She'd been feeling it more lately, an ache in her chest whenever she sat down after a long shift at the pizza joint, staring at the same four walls of her tiny apartment. Day in, day out. Nothing ever really changed. She was just getting by, too tired to do much else.

Maybe she was just bored. It had to be that, right? What else would drive someone to bring a wolf home with them on a whim? But there was something in her that liked the idea, the challenge of it. The thought of seeing if she could actually get away with keeping an animal in her flat – something wild, something that didn't belong – was almost... exciting. Like she was pushing the boundaries of what her life had become. Maybe it would break the monotony, give her something unexpected to look forward to.

She thought about her childhood Alsatian, how she used to play fetch with him in the yard, how he'd curl up at the foot of her bed at night. A real pet. Something she could take care of. Maybe that was what she wanted more than anything – to feel needed, to care for someone other than just herself. It had been so long since she'd had that.

She glanced at the wolf again. It wasn't exactly the same, not by a long shot, but it was close enough to make her wonder if this could be her way of filling the void. She didn't know what the hell she was doing, but for the first time in a long while, it felt like something was actually happening.

And even if it all went wrong – if she got caught and the landlord kicked her out – well, she figured the city had plenty of other rundown apartments with sky-high rent. At least she'd have a story to tell.

When they reached her apartment building, she fumbled with her keys in the dim light, hyperaware of the warm presence at her side. The lock finally clicked, and she pushed open the door, gesturing for her unexpected companion to enter. The wolf padded past her without hesitation, its fur brushing against her leg with a static-like tingle.

They stepped into the lift, and she pressed

the button for her floor. As the lift rose with a faint hum, she glanced down at the wolf, its reflective eyes fixed on the doors as if waiting. The moment the lift stopped, a soft ding broke the silence, and she led the way down a short hallway to her flat.

Inside her small kitchen, Toni filled her largest bowl with water, wincing at the way the pipes groaned. The wolf lapped at it eagerly while she conducted an archaeological dig through her cupboards, pushing aside ancient boxes of mac and cheese and dented soup cans until she found a tin of tuna. The pop of the can opening seemed unnaturally loud in the quiet apartment.

"Here you go," she said, tipping the contents onto a chipped plate and sliding it across the linoleum. The wolf descended on the meal hungrily, and Toni found herself wondering how long it had been since its last proper meal.

After finishing, the creature settled itself on the kitchen floor with surprising domesticity, arranging its large frame with an elegance that seemed out of place in her cramped apartment. Those remarkable eyes remained fixed on her, filled with an awareness that made her skin prickle.

"You seem like you've lived indoors before," Toni observed quietly.

The wolf's only response was to tilt its head slightly, but something in that gesture seemed almost too human.

Fighting back a yawn, she stepped out into the hallway and closed the door firmly, ensuring her strange guest would stay contained for the night. "Goodnight, big guy," she called through the door, her feet already carrying her towards the promise of sleep.

As Toni collapsed onto her bed, not even bothering to change out of her uniform, her last conscious thought was that she'd stepped into something bigger than a simple act of kindness to a stray. There was a weight to this encounter, a significance she couldn't grasp. As sleep pulled her under, a certainty lingered that tonight's decision would ripple outwards in ways she couldn't yet imagine.

Chapter Three

Toni surfaced from sleep to an unfamiliar sound filtering through her bedroom door. A rhythmic clinking echoed from the kitchen, metal against ceramic, accompanied by the soft sizzle of something on heat. For several foggy moments, she dismissed it as a remnant of some half-remembered dream, the kind that lingers in the space between sleeping and waking. Then the events of the previous night crashed back into her consciousness with the subtlety of a runaway freight train – the alley, the wolf, her impulsive decision to bring it home.

Heart thundering against her ribs like a trapped bird, Toni rolled out of bed with as much grace as her sleep-stiffened muscles would allow. As she crept towards the kitchen, her sock-clad feet silent against the worn carpet, her mind raced through possible scenarios, each worse than the last: shredded cabinet doors hanging from their hinges, her meagre food supplies strewn across the floor, maybe even a cornered wild animal ready to launch itself at her throat.

What she found instead stopped her dead in her tracks. A man stood at her ancient stove, his broad shoulders and muscular back on full display as he expertly flipped what appeared to be perfectly golden pancakes. He was shirtless, giving her an unobstructed view of intricate tattoos that wound down his arms like dark vines. But it was the network of old scars crisscrossing his skin that drew her attention – pale lines that spoke of violence and pain, creating a macabre roadmap across his flesh. His dark hair hung in wild tangles, as if he'd just rolled out of bed – though where he'd rolled out of was a mystery, since she distinctly remembered leaving a wolf in her kitchen, not a half-naked man with a talent for breakfast foods.

"Morning," he said casually, not bothering to turn around. His tone suggested this was a completely normal situation – just another day of breaking and entering to make breakfast for a stranger.

"Who the hell are you?" Toni demanded, recovering enough presence of mind to be on the defensive.

The man glanced over his shoulder, one eyebrow lifting in what might have been amusement. His profile was sharp, almost severe, but it was his eyes that made Toni's breath catch – they were exactly the same shade of amber as the wolf's, with that same unnerving intelligence burning in their depths.

"Relax," he said, his voice low and steady. "It's me. Well... the other me."

"What?" The word came out as more of a squeak than Toni would have liked, her brain struggling to process what he was implying.

He sighed, turning to face her fully. The front view was just as impressive as the back, his chest decorated with the same mix of tattoos and scars. But it was those eyes – those impossible, familiar eyes – that held her attention.

"No way?!" she said, her eyes widening with realisation. "You're the wolf?"

"Technically, I'm a wolf shifter," he corrected, turning back to rescue a pancake that was threatening to burn. The movement was fluid, almost predatory in its grace. "The name's Callen, by the way. Thanks for letting me crash here." He spoke as if this was a perfectly reasonable explanation, as casual as discussing the weather.

"This can't be real." Toni sagged against the door frame, her hand pressing against her forehead as if she could physically hold her scattered thoughts together. "I brought a stray animal home, not some guy who... who cooks pancakes!"

A smirk played at the corners of Callen's mouth as he added another perfectly browned pancake to the impressive stack beside the stove. "You didn't seem like the type to leave a helpless creature on the street," he observed. "So thanks for that, by the way." There was genuine gratitude in his voice, though it was partially masked by his casual demeanour.

Toni shook her head, trying to force the world to make sense again. The familiar smell of pancakes and coffee only made everything feel more surreal, like a dream that had wandered too far into reality. "Ok, assuming I'm not losing my mind – why are you making pancakes?"

"It's called gratitude," Callen said, sliding a plate loaded with pancakes onto her small kitchen table. Steam rose from them in appetising curls, and despite everything, Toni's traitor stomach growled. "I figured you deserved a proper breakfast after everything." He moved through her kitchen with surprising familiarity, locating cups and silverware as if he'd lived there for years instead of hours.

She stared at the plate, then back at him, feeling like she'd stumbled into some bizarre alternate reality where supernatural creatures showed up to make breakfast. "Gratitude? You're a talking wolf, dude! That's not something you just spring on someone with a side of syrup!" The hysteria in her voice was barely contained, threatening to bubble over into either laughter or screaming – she wasn't quite sure which.

Callen's expression sobered, the playful glint in his eyes dimming. He leaned against the counter, his posture subtly shifting from casual to guarded. "Look, I didn't mean to drag you into this. But... things are complicated right now. I didn't have anywhere else to go." There was a weight to his words that hadn't been there before, a hint of something darker lurking beneath the surface.

"Complicated how?" Toni pressed.

He hesitated, running a hand through his tangled hair. "Let's just say I've got some people looking for me. People who aren't exactly friendly." His jaw tightened, muscles working beneath the skin.

Toni crossed her arms, trying to maintain some semblance of control over the situation. "That doesn't explain how you ended up as a wolf in the middle of the city."

Callen's expression darkened further, his fingers absently tracing one of the tattoos on his arm. "It's these runes," he said finally, drawing her attention to a series of faint markings she hadn't noticed before, barely visible beneath the more obvious artwork. They seemed to shift slightly when she tried to focus on them, like trying to read underwater. "They're messing with my shifting abilities."

"Runes?" Toni frowned, taking an unconscious step closer to examine the strange markings. "Like magic?" The word felt ridiculous coming out of her mouth, especially standing in her cramped kitchen with the smell of pancakes in the air.

"Yeah. Magic." His tone was flat, but when his amber eyes met hers, she saw something that looked dangerously like desperation. "Someone put them on me. Long story. It's complicated." The admission seemed to cost him something, his shoulders tensing as if expecting judgment or disbelief.

Toni pressed her fingers against her temples, trying to ward off the headache she could feel building. Nothing in her life – not her dead-end job, not her struggling bank account, not even her occasionally questionable life choices – had prepared her for this moment. But something in Callen's voice, something raw and vulnerable beneath his casual exterior, made it impossible to simply dismiss him as a hallucination or a very elaborate practical joke.

"So, what do you want from me?" she asked finally, surprising herself with how steady her voice sounded.

"Help," Callen said simply, the word hanging in the air between them. "I can't figure out how to fix this on my own, and I don't exactly have a lot of friends in the city. You seem... capable."

Toni couldn't help but snort, the sound sharp with disbelief. "Capable of what? I work at a pizza joint and can barely afford my rent." The admission stung, but it was true.

"Capable of surviving," he countered, his gaze steady and uncomfortably perceptive. "That's more than most people." The words hit closer to home than she would have liked, recognising something in her that she rarely acknowledged herself.

She opened her mouth to argue, then closed it again. Much as she hated to admit it, he wasn't wrong. She'd been surviving on her own for years, keeping her head above water through sheer determination and a stubborn refusal to give up.

"Fine," she said at last, the word coming out like a surrender. "But if you're staying here, there are rules. No shifting into a wolf and shedding all over my couch. And you're doing your share of the dishes." The normalcy of the demands felt almost comical given the circumstances, but they helped ground her in reality.

A grin broke across Callen's face, relief sparking in those extraordinary eyes. "Deal," he said, and for a moment, she caught a glimpse of the wolf in his smile – wild and dangerous, but somehow trustworthy all the same.

Toni sighed heavily, grabbing a fork and stabbing it into the stack of pancakes with more force than necessary. As she drowned them in syrup, she couldn't shake the feeling that she'd just signed up for something far more demanding than providing shelter to a stray. Whatever it was, it felt too late to back out now. The pancakes, at least, were perfect – though that was small consolation for having her world turned upside down before she'd even had her morning coffee.

Chapter Four

The day unfolded like a fever dream, reality bending at the edges where the ordinary met the impossible. By the time Toni had to leave for her shift at Pizza Time, Callen had made himself completely at home on her threadbare couch, sprawled across it with casual grace as he channel-surfed through the static-filled offerings of her ancient television set. The sight was so jarringly domestic that she had to remind herself that less than twenty-four hours ago, he'd been a wolf in an alley. She'd left him with a warning that tried to sound stern but probably fell short – "Don't touch anything or cause trouble" – like telling a hurricane not to make a mess. As she locked her apartment door, she couldn't shake the feeling that she was leaving behind a grenade with its pin hanging by a thread, just waiting for the slightest jostle to explode.

The familiar assault of the place hit her the moment she pushed through Pizza Time's doors – rancid grease, overcooked cheese, and the peculiar metallic tang of the industrial ovens that never quite cooled down. Greg was holding court, his reedy voice raised in what he probably thought was constructive criticism as he spoke to a new hire. The poor kid – couldn't have been older than sixteen – had that glazed look of someone discovering just how much customer service could drain the soul. His name tag was still pristine, unmarked by the grease stains that would inevitably claim it. Toni could already tell he wouldn't last the week.

She jammed her polyester visor onto her head, tucking stray strands of blue hair beneath it, and threw herself into the mindless routine of her shift. But even as her hands moved through the familiar motions – stretching dough, layering toppings, boxing pizzas – her thoughts kept circling back to her impossible guest. What kind of trouble follows a man who can turn into a wolf? And who exactly were these "people" looking for him? The questions nagged at her like an itch she couldn't scratch, making every minute of her shift feel like an hour.

The day dragged itself along like a wounded animal. Every burnt crust and cold delivery complaint grated against her nerves, each customer's face blurring into the next until they became a single, endless stream of disappointment. When the last pizza finally found its way into its box and the temperamental neon sign sputtered into darkness, Toni was out the door before Greg could finish saying "goodnight", her feet carrying her the three miles home at a pace just short of running.

The walk felt stretched somehow, as if the city itself had expanded while she wasn't looking. The streets were unusually quiet, the typical urban cacophony muted under a blanket of nighttime fog that had rolled in. Even the traffic seemed subdued, car engines purring rather than roaring, horns honking with less enthusiasm than usual. Or maybe it was just her exhaustion colouring everything in more muted tones, her mind too preoccupied with thoughts of Callen to notice the city's usual vitality. Questions tumbled through her head like clothes in a dryer. What kind of trouble had she invited into her life? Who was hunting him? And, more importantly, would they find their way to her door?

By the time she reached her building, her keys were already in her hand, but she hesitated before inserting them into the lock. The moment felt loaded with possibility – would she open her apartment door to find the place trashed? Would Callen even still be there? Or worse, would she find something else entirely, something that explained why people might be hunting a man who could turn into a wolf?

"Please don't let it be a disaster," she muttered under her breath, a prayer to whatever deity might be listening to minimum wage workers and their questionable life choices.

She stepped into the lift and jabbed the button for her floor, her foot tapping anxiously as it ascended with a faint hum. The ride felt agonisingly long, each second giving her imagination more room to conjure worst-case scenarios waiting behind her apartment door.

The lock clicked, and she pushed the door open with the cautious optimism of someone poking a suspicious package. The scene that greeted her was so startlingly normal that for a moment, she wondered if she'd walked into the wrong apartment. Not only was everything intact, but Callen was in her kitchen again, wielding a knife with the confident precision of a professional chef. Vegetables fell beneath his blade in perfectly even pieces, each movement fluid and practiced. The domestic normality of it felt almost more surreal than finding him cooking pancakes that morning.

"I figured you'd be hungry," he said without looking up, his voice casual as if this was their hundredth meal together rather than their second. Steam rose from a wok she didn't even know she owned, carrying the promise of actual food rather than reheated pizza. "I hope you like stir-fry."

Toni blinked slowly, her brain too tired to generate proper suspicion. Her bag slid from her shoulder and landed with a thud by the door as she made her way to the couch, collapsing onto it with all the grace of a fallen tree. The familiar springs creaked beneath her weight as she sank into the worn cushions. "This is the weirdest week of my life," she announced to the ceiling.

Callen's chuckle floated over from the kitchen, warm and surprisingly genuine. "You're handling it better than most people would." The rhythmic sound of his chopping never faltered, creating a strangely soothing backdrop to their conversation.

"That's because I haven't had time to freak out yet." She closed her eyes, letting the aromatic blend of garlic, ginger, and soy sauce wash over her. The smell was mouthwatering, making the pizza she'd grabbed during her break seem like a distant, greasy memory. "So, are you going to tell me what's really going on? Or are you just going to keep cooking and hoping I don't ask?"

The steady rhythm of the knife against the cutting board stopped abruptly, leaving a silence broken only by the gentle sizzle of vegetables in the wok. Toni opened her eyes to find Callen had set down his knife, his muscular frame now leaning against the counter. His amber eyes met hers with an intensity that made her want to look away, but she held his gaze.

"Fine," he said finally, the word carrying the weight of surrender. "You deserve to know."

Toni sat up straighter, exhaustion temporarily forgotten in the face of potential answers. "Start with the runes. What do they do?" She tried to keep her voice steady, confident, as if she discussed magical tattoos every day after work.

"They're a mark of control," Callen said, his voice tight with barely contained emotion. One hand absently traced the faint markings on his arm, as if they pained him. "The alpha who put them on me wanted to keep me weak – unable to shift at will and less able to fight back. I've managed to shift back into my human form, but it's... unstable." The admission seemed to cost him something, his jaw clenching against words left unsaid.

"Why would someone do that to you?" Toni frowned, trying to wrap her mind around the concept of magical restraints. It seemed almost medieval, like something out of a dark fairy tale.

"Because I'm an omega," he said simply, the words falling into the space between them like stones into still water.

She blinked, her tired brain struggling to make connections. "An omega? Like... in a pack?" The word felt strange on her tongue, too primal for her small apartment with its flickering fluorescent kitchen light and dripping tap.

Callen nodded, his expression guarded. "Yeah. It's a hierarchy thing. Alphas at the top, omegas at the bottom. Some packs treat it like tradition. Others..." He shrugged, but the casual gesture couldn't quite mask the tension in his shoulders. "Let's just say not all omegas are treated equally."

"And your pack?" The question slipped out before she could stop it, drawn by the darkness lurking behind his words.

"They're not my pack anymore," Callen said, his jaw tightening until she could see the muscles working beneath his skin. "I left. They didn't take it well. The alpha – Rogan – he made sure to make it clear that I had betrayed him." The understatement hung in the air like smoke, acrid with unspoken violence.

Toni leaned back into the couch, letting his words settle over her like a heavy blanket. She might not know anything about shifters or magic, but she recognised the tone of someone who'd escaped something toxic. It was the same edge she'd heard in her own voice when she'd finally walked away from her family's expectations. Something about Callen's carefully controlled expression made her chest tight with recognition – he'd been through hell, and he was still picking his way through the aftermath.

"Ok," she said slowly, choosing her words with care. "So, these runes – how do we get rid of them?" The "we" slipped out naturally, though she wasn't quite sure when she'd decided to commit to helping him with this.

"That's the problem," Callen said, frustration bleeding into his voice as he turned back to the wok, stirring its contents with more force than necessary. "I don't know. I've been trying to figure it out, but I'm out of leads. I was hoping you might be able to help."

Toni raised an eyebrow, unable to keep the scepticism from her voice. "What makes you think I know anything about magic?"

"You're resourceful," Callen said simply, as if that explained everything. After a pause, he added quietly, "And I don't have anyone else."

Toni sighed heavily, running a hand through her hair and grimacing when her fingers caught on tangles left by the polyester visor. "You're lucky I don't have a social life," she grumbled, "or I'd tell you to find someone else to play detective."

A smirk tugged at the corner of Callen's mouth, his amber eyes warming with something that might have been amusement. "You're not as tough as you let on, are you?"

"Don't push your luck," she warned, but the words came out softer than intended, lacking their usual edge. The smell of cooking and the strange comfort of company after a long shift had worn down her defences more than she cared to admit.

She studied him for a moment longer, taking in the contradiction of his presence – a powerful supernatural being making dinner in her tiny kitchen, hiding from unknown threats behind her deadbolt lock and peeling wallpaper.

With another sigh, she grabbed a battered notebook and pen from the cluttered coffee table. "Fine. Let's start with what you know about these runes. Any books or symbols we can cross-reference?"

Something in Callen's expression softened, gratitude flickering across his features like sunlight through leaves. "Thanks, Toni. I mean it." The sincerity in his voice made her uncomfortable in a way she couldn't quite name.

"Yeah, yeah," she muttered, flipping open the notebook with more force than necessary. The familiar action of preparing to take notes helped ground her in reality, even as that reality stretched to accommodate magic.

Chapter Five

The next morning, Toni found herself wedged between the towering oak shelves of the local library, her fingers tracing the spine of yet another ancient book whose gilded title promised answers about the occult. The musty scent of aged paper filled her nose as she squinted at the faded text, trying to ignore the way her legs ached from standing. She'd been at this for hours already, and the growing pile of rejected volumes beside her feet wasn't exactly inspiring confidence. Callen was with her, though his presence was about as subtle as a wolf in a chicken coop – which, given what she now knew about him, wasn't entirely off the mark.

His massive frame dominated the narrow aisle, drawing sideways glances from every patron who passed by. Not that Toni could blame them; with his broad shoulders nearly brushing both shelves and those unnaturally amber eyes scanning the room like a predator marking territory, he wasn't exactly blending into the quiet academic atmosphere. The leather jacket and combat boots probably weren't helping either.

"This is a terrible plan," Toni muttered under her breath, flipping another page with more force than necessary. The paper crackled in protest as her eyes skimmed over yet another useless paragraph about crystal healing and moon phases. Nothing even remotely close to the angular, almost tribal-looking marks that decorated Callen's skin. "We're basically looking for a needle in a haystack made of new-age nonsense and medieval superstition."

"Got a better idea?" Callen's deep voice carried from where he leaned against the shelves, managing to look simultaneously relaxed and coiled for action. The wood creaked ominously under his weight, and Toni shot him a warning look. The last thing they needed was to explain a collapsed bookshelf to the already suspicious library staff.

"Not yet," she admitted reluctantly, snapping the book shut with a dull thud that earned her a disapproving look from a nearby student. "But I have to say, spending my precious day off diving into the metaphysical studies section wasn't exactly what I had planned. I was thinking more along the lines of coffee, rubbish TV, and absolutely zero research into magical tattoo removal."

"You're doing great," he said, and she could hear the smile in his voice without even looking up. The amusement in his tone only irritated her more, though she couldn't entirely explain why. Maybe because he seemed to find her frustration entertaining, or maybe because his casual confidence made her feel like she was somehow failing at a test she hadn't signed up for.

She shot him a glare that would have withered a lesser man before reaching for another tome. This one was particularly ancient, bound in cracked leather that felt brittle beneath her fingertips. The cover was worn smooth in places, and the spine bore no title – just a series of deep creases that spoke of countless openings over what must have been centuries. The smell of mildew and decay wafted up as she carefully parted the pages, making her nose wrinkle.

But as she diligently engaged, something caught her eye that made her breath catch. There, rendered in faded but still visible black ink, was a series of intricate symbols that made her pulse quicken. The designs weren't exactly like the ones she'd seen etched into Callen's skin, but the similarity was undeniable – the same sharp angles, the same flowing curves that seemed to catch and hold the eye.

"Hey," she said, her voice dropping to barely more than a whisper. "Take a look at this." She held the book out towards him, careful not to let the fragile spine crack further. Her fingers had left slight smudges on the yellowed pages, and she felt a pang of guilt for marking something so old.

Callen pushed off from the shelf and moved closer, his presence suddenly filling her personal space with warmth and that strange wild scent that seemed to cling to him – like pine needles and wood smoke. He took the book from her hands, his large fingers surprisingly gentle with the delicate pages.

His expression darkened as he studied the symbols, the amber colour of his eyes seeming to intensify.

"Yes, they're binding runes," he said after a long moment, his voice pitched low and grim. The playful edge from earlier had vanished entirely. "Just like the ones you've seen on me. They're used in rituals designed to suppress magic or keep someone under control. Like a magical cage." The last words came out as almost a growl, and Toni noticed his fingers tightening on the book's edges.

"Well, that's thoroughly cheerful," she said, crossing her arms tightly across her chest to suppress a shiver. The temperature in the library suddenly seemed to have dropped several degrees. "Please tell me it at least has instructions for getting rid of them. You know, like a magical key for the magical cage?"

Callen's eyes moved rapidly across the text surrounding the symbols, his jaw tightening with each line. "There's mention of a counterspell," he said finally, frustration evident in every word. "But the actual instructions aren't here. Looks like whoever wrote this was more interested in how to imprison someone with dark magic rather than how to undo it."

"Of course," Toni muttered, resisting the urge to kick the nearby shelf. "Because why would anything about this situation be straightforward or helpful? That would be far too convenient."

She was about to launch into a more detailed complaint about the universe's apparent vendetta against them when movement at the end of the aisle caught her attention. The librarian – a stern-looking woman with steel-grey hair pulled back in a tight bun – had materialised like a disapproving ghost. Her sharp eyes narrowed as she took in the scene: the pile of books on the floor, the ancient tome in Callen's hands, their suspicious huddle in the occult section.

"Excuse me," the woman said, her voice carrying that special blend of politeness and authority that only career librarians seemed able to master. "May I ask what exactly you're looking for? This section contains some very valuable reference materials."

Toni felt herself freeze, suddenly acutely aware of how suspicious they must look. Her mind raced for a plausible explanation that didn't involve wolves or dark magic, but before she could cobble one together, Callen stepped smoothly into action.

He turned towards the librarian with a smile that transformed his entire face, somehow managing to look both charming and completely innocent – a feat Toni wouldn't have thought possible for someone his size. "Just doing some research for a historical fiction project," he said, his voice warm and professional. "We're being very careful with the materials, I assure you. We won't be much longer."

The librarian's stern expression wavered under the full force of that smile, and after a moment that felt much longer than it probably was, she gave a small nod and turned away. Her sensible shoes made soft squeaking sounds on the linoleum as she retreated.

"Nice save," Toni whispered once the woman was out of earshot. "Where did that come from?"

"Years of practice," Callen replied, returning the book to her with a slight shrug. "When you live on society's edges, you learn to blend in when necessary." There was something in his tone that hinted at darker stories beneath the simple statement, but Toni decided that was probably a conversation for another time.

They spent another painstaking hour combing through the remaining books, piecing together fragments of information like some kind of mystical jigsaw puzzle. By the time they finally admitted defeat and headed for the exit, Toni's bag was stuffed with photocopies and hastily scribbled notes, and her head was swimming with half-understood terms and cryptic warnings about magical backlash.

The walk back to her flat was quiet, both of them lost in their own thoughts. The late afternoon sun cast long shadows across the pavement, and Toni found herself studying Callen's as they walked, half expecting to see something inhuman in its shape. But it looked perfectly normal – just the silhouette of a very tall, broad-shouldered man. She wasn't sure if that was reassuring or not.

Back in the relative safety of her small flat, Toni cleared her coffee table with a sweep of her arm, sending magazines and old mail cascading to the floor. She spread out their collected research materials, trying to impose some sort of order on the chaos of photocopied pages and hurried notes. Callen paced the length of the living area like a caged animal, his agitation filling the small space until she could practically taste it in the air.

"Ok," she said finally, holding up a particularly worn photocopy that she'd marked with several exclamation points. "This one might actually be useful. It mentions a specific ritual for breaking binding runes." She squinted at her own handwriting, which had grown increasingly messy as the day wore on. "Though I have to say, the requirements seem... intense. There's a lot about something called a spirit anchor?"

"Great," Callen's voice dripped with sarcasm as he paused his pacing to look over her shoulder. "Because complex magic rituals always end well. I can't imagine anything going wrong with that plan."

Toni ignored his commentary, though she had to assume he had a point. She circled the term "spirit anchor" with her red pen, adding a large question mark beside it. "I'm guessing from your tone that you know what this means? Because right now I'm picturing something like a magical boat anchor, which seems impractical."

"It's an object tied to someone's essence," Callen said, finally dropping onto her couch. The furniture creaked alarmingly under his weight. "Something deeply personal, usually chosen during a pack binding ritual. I assume the runes must be connected to it." His voice had taken on that forced neutrality that she was learning meant he was trying to hide strong emotions. He leaned forward, elbows on his knees, staring at the floor as if the answers to every problem might appear there. "For me," he continued after a long pause, "it's a bear's tooth necklace – a large bear tooth, strung on a thick black thread. My mother gave it to me when I was a pup. She said it was a symbol of strength and resilience, a reminder of who I am, even when things feel impossible."

Toni stayed silent, letting him speak.

"I wore it every day," Callen said, his tone softening with nostalgia. "Through every scrape, every hunt, every fight. It was... part of me." His jaw tightened, and his hands clenched into fists. "When Rogan suggested using it for the binding ritual, I didn't even hesitate. At the time, it felt right. I was proud to be part of the pack, to prove my loyalty. Giving him the necklace wasn't a sacrifice – it was an honour." He exhaled sharply, shaking his head. "I regret it now. I was too blind, too eager to please. I thought I was securing my place in the pack. Instead, I must have handed Rogan the power to keep me there, whether I wanted to stay or not." The regret in his voice was unmistakable, a deep ache that made Toni wince in sympathy.

"So," Toni said slowly, leaning back against the couch and running a hand through her dishevelled hair, "we need to get hold of the necklace because that's your spirit anchor – the specific object that keeps you connected to the pack against your will." She paused, already knowing she wasn't going to like the answer. "Any idea where it might be?"

Callen was quiet for a long moment, his expression unreadable in the fading daylight that filtered through her cheap curtains. When he finally spoke, his voice was barely above a whisper. "It's probably still with the pack," he admitted, the weight of unspoken history in those words making Toni's chest tighten. "Rogan would have kept it somewhere safe. Somewhere I can't reach it."

"Of course," Toni muttered, letting her head fall back against the chair. "Because nothing about this whole situation could possibly be simple or straightforward. That would go against whatever cosmic law seems to be governing my life lately."

Callen's amber eyes met hers, his gaze intense and searching. "You can walk away from all of this if you want to," he said quietly. "I mean it. This isn't your fight."

"Too late," she said, surprising herself with the firmness in her voice. "I'm already invested now. Besides, I'm not about to let you run off and get yourself killed trying to handle this alone. I'd feel guilty."

A hint of a smile tugged at the corners of his mouth, softening his features. "You're not nearly as tough and detached as you pretend to be, you know that?"

"Don't push your luck," she shot back, though she couldn't quite keep the answering smile from her voice. "I can still change my mind and leave you to figure this out on your own."

They both knew she was lying, but Callen was kind enough not to call her on it. Instead, they lapsed into contemplative silence as the last rays of sunlight faded, leaving them reliant on the kitchen's strip lighting. The enormity of what lay ahead settled over them like a heavy blanket – they had a lead, yes, but following it meant confronting Callen's past, something she suspected was dangerous in more ways than one.

As Toni stared at the scattered papers that represented their day's work, she found herself wondering, not for the first time, how her life had taken such a sharp turn into the supernatural. More importantly, she wondered if she was truly ready for whatever lay at the end of this path she'd chosen to walk. The rational part of her brain was screaming that she was in way over her head, but something deeper – something that resonated with the determined look in

Callen's eyes – told her that she was on the right track.

Whether that was a good thing remained to be seen.

Chapter Six

T he next day dawned with a biting autumn chill. Toni stood at her window, watching her breath fog the glass as thoughts of their hastily constructed plan gnawed at her mind. After hours of debate and planning well into the night, they had finally agreed on what needed to be done. They had to retrieve Callen's spirit anchor – the bear's tooth necklace that, according to their research, held the key to breaking his binding. The problem was that the anchor was almost certainly in the possession of his former pack. And based on Callen's terse explanations, they weren't exactly the type to welcome visitors with tea and cookies.

The metal of the pocket knife she had decided to keep about her person felt impossibly cold as she strapped it to her belt, its weight against her hip both reassuring and underwhelming. Toni had spent nearly an hour staring at it on her bedside table before making the decision. The thought of actually carrying a weapon made her stomach clench.

She wasn't fooling herself – a three-inch blade wasn't going to do much against a pack of wolves if things went sideways. But it was better than nothing, and right now, "better than nothing" was about the best she could manage. She caught her reflection in the mirror as she grabbed her backpack – pale face, dark circles under her eyes, hair hastily pulled back in a messy ponytail. She looked exactly like someone who was about to do something incredibly stupid.

Callen stood by her front door like a statue carved from tension, his usual easy-going demeanour replaced by something harder and more dangerous. His amber eyes had taken on a predatory gleam that reminded her, with uncomfortable clarity, exactly what he was. He'd dressed for trouble – dark clothes, sturdy boots, and an expression that suggested he was already preparing for the worst.

"You ready?" Toni asked, though the question felt absurd as soon as it left her lips. How does one really get ready to raid a den of wolves? She shouldered her backpack, trying to project a confidence she definitely didn't feel.

"As ready as I'll ever be," he replied, his voice carrying an edge she hadn't heard before.

They emerged into the city's morning rush, weaving through crowds of commuters who remained blissfully unaware that anything unusual was happening. Toni found herself studying their faces, wondering how many of them might actually be supernatural creatures hiding in plain sight. After all, if wolf shifters were real, what else was out there? The thought made her head spin, so she focused instead on following Callen's lead as they navigated through the labyrinth of streets and alleyways she'd once thought she knew so well.

Their destination was a secluded industrial zone on the city's outskirts – the kind of place that seemed purpose-built for nefarious activities. As they walked, the crowds thinned and the buildings grew increasingly dilapidated, like the city itself was gradually giving up.

"Tell me about them," Toni said, breaking the tense silence that had fallen between them. Her voice sounded too loud in the empty street.

"The pack?" Callen's tone carried a wariness that made her stomach clench. He spoke the word "pack" like it was something sharp in his mouth.

"Yeah. I think I deserve to know what we're walking into." She tried to keep her voice steady, matter-of-fact. "Especially since there's a good chance they'll try to kill us."

He was quiet for so long that she thought he might not answer. When he finally spoke, each word seemed carefully chosen. "They're not all bad people. Most of them are just... lost. Looking for belonging. The pack offers that, along with protection and power." He paused, his jaw tightening. "But the alpha – Rogan – is something else entirely. He's controlling, manipulative. Brutal when he thinks someone's stepped out of line. When I left, it wasn't just about rejecting the hierarchy or wanting independence. It was about survival."

"Sounds like a real charmer," Toni muttered, trying to mask her growing unease with sarcasm. "Let me guess – he's not the type to respond well to polite requests?"

Callen's lips twitched in what might have been a smile if it hadn't been so devoid of humour. "He won't let go of what he considers his property. And in his mind, that includes both me and the spirit anchor. Especially since the anchor is what gives him control over me."

They arrived at the industrial district as the sun began its descent towards the horizon, painting the sky in shades of amber and blood red that felt uncomfortably appropriate. The complex was a sprawling wasteland of abandoned warehouses and forgotten machinery, everything covered in a thick layer of rust and decay. The air carried the acrid tang of old oil and corroded metal, mixed with something else – something wild and dangerous that made the hair on the back of Toni's neck stand up.

"This is it," Callen said quietly, nodding towards a massive structure that looked like it had been abandoned mid-apocalypse.

The windows were mostly broken, their jagged edges catching the dying sunlight like teeth. The walls were a canvas of graffiti, and the whole building seemed to lean slightly, as if tired of standing.

"Great," Toni said, her fingers tightening on her backpack straps until her knuckles went white. "Really loving the ambiance. Very "horror movie waiting to happen"." She swallowed hard, forcing down her fear. "So, what's the actual plan here? Besides the general "get in, grab the necklace, try not to die" outline we discussed?"

"Stay behind me," Callen said, his voice dropping to barely more than a whisper. His eyes were scanning the building, picking out details she probably couldn't even see. "If things go wrong – if I tell you to run – you get out. Don't wait for me, don't try to help. Just run."

"Not a chance," Toni said, the words coming out fiercer than she'd intended. "We're in this together, remember? I didn't come all this way to abandon you to your psycho ex-pack."

Callen turned to look at her then, and something in his expression made her breath catch. It was a mixture of gratitude, fear, and something else she couldn't quite name. But he didn't argue, which she counted as a win. Instead, he took a step back and began to change.

The transformation was both beautiful and terrifying – a fluid ripple of movement that seemed to defy the laws of physics. One moment he was human, the next he was a massive black wolf with familiar amber eyes. His fur seemed to absorb the fading light, making him nearly invisible in the growing shadows. Toni found herself momentarily transfixed, despite having seen Callen in his wolf form before. It was the kind of thing that her brain still struggled to accept as real, even as it happened right in front of her.

They approached the building together, moving as quietly as possible across the debris-strewn ground. The entrance they chose was a side door that hung askew on its hinges, groaning softly in the evening breeze.

Inside, the air was thick with dust and the musty smell of abandonment. Their footsteps – Toni's quiet boots and Callen's near-silent paws – seemed impossibly loud in the stillness.

The sound of voices reached them, echoing from somewhere deeper in the building. They were low and guttural, carrying undertones that seemed more animal than human. Callen froze, his ears swivelling towards the sound like radar dishes. Toni followed his lead, trying to control her breathing as they crept forward.

They emerged onto a kind of mezzanine overlooking a vast open space below. The scene that greeted them made Toni's heart skip several beats. A group of shifters occupied the centre of the room, their forms flickering between human and wolf as they moved and spoke, as if they couldn't quite decide which shape to wear. The effect was deeply unsettling. A fire burned in what looked like an old oil drum, casting dancing shadows on the walls and illuminating their gathering place.

But what really caught Toni's attention was the wooden box – just a tad smaller than her backpack – situated on a crude altar of broken pallets and cinder blocks. It was surrounded by carefully drawn symbols that she recognised from their research – binding runes, power containment circles, and other markings that practically hummed with malevolent purpose.

"There," Callen's voice whispered in her mind, seeming surprisingly natural. "The anchor's inside. I can feel it with every fibre of my being."

"Of course it is," Toni uttered under her breath, barely audible even to herself. "Right in the middle of everything, surrounded by the scary magic symbols. Because why would it be somewhere convenient, like by the door?"

Her attention was drawn to movement below as one of the shifters approached the box. He was massive, even in human form, his towering frame clad in a dark shirt that strained against the breadth of his muscular shoulders. His sharp features seemed carved from granite, all hard angles and ridges, giving him the appearance of someone who had been sculpted for the sole purpose of intimidation. His jet-black hair was cropped close to his skull, accentuating the stark lines of his face, and his jaw tightened as if he was perpetually on the verge of snapping. Everything about him radiated authority and barely contained anger, a coiled spring ready to explode at the slightest provocation. This had to be Rogan. Just looking at him made Toni's pulse quicken and her instincts scream for her to run in the opposite direction.

"What now?" she whispered, her voice tight with tension. Their planning hadn't really extended past getting inside, and she was starting to think that had been a serious oversight.

Callen's amber eyes met hers, and she could have sworn she saw a glint of what might have been apology in them. His voice echoed clearly in her mind, deliberate and controlled: "Distraction."

Before she could process what that meant – before she could even think to object – he was moving. He launched himself from their hiding place with explosive force, his massive black form sailing through the air towards the gathered shifters. His snarl echoed off the walls like crackles of thunder, and chaos erupted instantly.

The pack scattered in all directions, some shifting into wolf form in mid-motion while others scrambled for weapons that had been hidden around the room. The fire barrel toppled, sending burning debris skittering across the floor and casting wild shadows everywhere.

Toni didn't have time to think, which was probably good because thinking would have involved recognising how absolutely insane this situation was. Instead, she moved on pure adrenaline, sprinting down the nearest stairs towards the box. Her footsteps were lost in the cacophony of snarls, shouts, and bodies colliding.

She was within arm's reach of the box when movement caught her eye – a shifter lunging towards her with impossible speed, his features already elongating into something horrifyingly between human and wolf. His claws gleamed in the scattered firelight, reaching for her throat.

Pure instinct took over. Toni ducked and lunged, coming up with her pocket knife already slashing in a wide arc. She felt the blade connect, heard the shifter's howl of pain and surprise as she sliced a long gash across his forearm. It wasn't a deadly wound, but it bought her the precious seconds she needed.

She quickly pocketed her knife and grabbed the box, nearly dropping it in her haste. "Got it!" she shouted, her voice cracking with fear and exertion as she clutched it to her chest and began backing towards the nearest exit.

All around her was mayhem. Callen was a blur of black fur and snapping teeth, somehow holding off multiple attackers at once with a ferocity that was terrifying to witness. Even Rogan seemed hesitant to approach him directly, instead circling and looking for an opening.

"Toni, go!" Callen's voice filled her head, sharp with command and desperation. "Get out now!"

But she couldn't do it, couldn't leave him here to face this alone. Instead, she spotted a length of metal pipe among the debris and snatched it up with her free hand, wielding it like a club as another shifter tried to circle around behind her. "Not without you!" she shouted back, swinging the pipe in a wide arc that connected with a satisfying crack.

Callen must have realised she wasn't leaving because he suddenly changed tactics. With a growl that seemed to shake the very foundations of the building, he lunged at Rogan directly. The alpha tried to dodge but wasn't quite fast enough – Callen's massive shoulder caught him in the chest, sending him flying backwards into several other pack members.

In the moment of confusion that followed, Callen spun and sprinted towards her. Together, they ran for the exit, Toni still clutching the box while trying not to drop the pipe, which somehow seemed more reassuring than the knife. Behind them, she could hear the sounds of pursuit, but Callen seemed to know exactly where he was going. He led them through a maze of corridors and storage rooms, taking turns that somehow always seemed to work in their favour.

They didn't stop running until they were several blocks away, hidden in the shadows of an alley between two abandoned buildings. Toni's lungs were on fire, and every muscle in her body screamed in protest as she carefully set the box down. Her legs gave out and she slid down the rough brick wall, not even caring about the scrapes it left on her back.

"Please," she said, gasping between desperate breaths, "please tell me that was worth it." She could feel her hands shaking as the adrenaline began to wear off to make way for exhaustion.

Callen shifted back into his human form beside her, his face ghostly pale in the dim light but his eyes burning with determination. He knelt next to the box, his hands hovering over the runes carved into its wooden surface. A slight tremor ran through his fingers – whether from exhaustion or emotion, she couldn't tell.

"It's in here," he said, his voice thick with something that might have been relief or perhaps fear. "I can feel it. The spirit anchor. Just what we need." He looked up at her then, and the intensity in his eyes made her breath catch. "Thank you. For not leaving me. Even though you should have."

Toni managed a weak laugh that might have been slightly hysterical. "Yeah, well, apparently I make terrible life choices. Add it to the list." She let her head fall back against the wall, looking up at the strip of sky visible between the buildings. The stars were just beginning to appear, twinkling innocently as if the world hadn't just tilted even further off its axis.

Chapter Seven

Back in the relative safety of her flat, Toni stood in the tiny kitchen, clutching a mug of instant coffee like it was a lifeline. She'd briefly considered something stronger, but given what they were about to attempt, she figured keeping a clear head was probably wise. The bitter liquid had gone cold while she'd been staring at the box, but she barely noticed.

The stolen box sat on her coffee table. In the harsh light of the flat, she could finally get a good look at it. The wood was dark with age, its surface a maze of scratches and scuff marks that spoke of years of rough handling. But it was the runes that drew her attention – intricate symbols carved deep into the wood that seemed to pulse with a subtle light that shouldn't have been possible. Sometimes, when she looked at them from the corner of her eye, they appeared to writhe and shift like living things.

They'd already agreed not to open it. Callen had been so damn certain that the bear's tooth necklace was inside that Toni hadn't even thought to question it. She had seen the conviction in his eyes, the way he seemed to almost ache with the knowledge that the object most tied to him was so close, yet still out of reach. As much as Callen would have loved to see it again – to hold the necklace his mother had given him when he was just a pup – he didn't dare. "We can't risk it," he'd said, his voice tense with restrained emotion. "Not until we're absolutely confident about the ritual. If we mess this up, if I lose control or we activate the runes in the wrong way, things could spiral fast. And I can't... I can't let that happen."

As Toni stared at the box, she knew he wasn't just protecting himself. He was protecting her too – from whatever darkness was bound up in that ancient wood and the runes etched into its surface.

"So," she said finally, her voice cutting through the heavy silence that had settled over them, "what now?" The question felt inadequate given the situation, but she needed to say something to break the tension.

Callen sat cross-legged on her threadbare carpet, his shirt still dark with sweat from their earlier escapade. He didn't answer immediately, his unnaturally amber eyes fixed on the box with an intensity that made her wonder if he was seeing something she couldn't. When he finally turned to look at her, his expression was grim enough to make her stomach clench.

"Now comes the hard part," he said, his voice low and serious.

Toni let out a sharp laugh that held very little humour. "Harder than stealing it from a pack of angry shifters? Because I've got to tell you, that felt pretty hard at the time." She absently rubbed her shoulder where she'd hit the wall during their escape, knowing the bruise would be spectacular by morning.

A small smile flickered across Callen's face, but it didn't reach his eyes. "Breaking the bond isn't as simple as destroying the object.

The spirit anchor is connected to the runes, yes, but it's also fundamentally tied to me – to my essence, my life force, whatever you want to call it. If we make a mistake in severing those connections..." He trailed off, leaving the sentence hanging in the air like a guillotine blade.

"You could die?" Toni finished for him, setting her mug down on the counter with more force than necessary. The sharp sound made them both flinch. She'd suspected as much, but stating it so plainly made it feel terrifyingly real.

"Yeah," Callen admitted, running a hand through his dishevelled hair. "But if we don't try, the runes will keep doing what they were designed to do – draining my power, my autonomy. There will come a point where I'm not able to shift anymore. After that, I'll become weaker until one day I perish."

Toni pinched the bridge of her nose, feeling the beginnings of a headache building behind her eyes. The enormity of the situation pressed down on her almost physically, making it hard to think clearly. "Ok," she said, forcing herself to be practical.

"So how do we not screw it up? Please tell me all those hours in the library gave us something concrete to work with."

Callen reached underneath the small coffee table and grabbed their collection of photocopies and hastily scribbled notes from the library. He spread them across the floor with careful precision, like he was laying out the pieces of a particularly complicated puzzle. His finger came to rest on one page in particular, tapping it for emphasis.

"This ritual," he said, his voice taking on an intensity that made her pay close attention. "It's dangerous, and there's a lot that could go wrong, but it's the best shot we've got."

Toni moved closer, crouching down to study the page he was indicating.

"Salt, iron, moonlight..." Callen read aloud, his voice getting progressively higher with each item until he reached the last one. "And blood."

"Blood?!"

Callen's grim expression was answer enough, but he elaborated anyway. "The runes are literally bound to my life force. It says here that blood magic is the only thing powerful enough to break that kind of connection."

"Whose blood?" Toni asked, though the sinking feeling in her chest told her she already knew the answer. She just needed to hear him say it.

"Mine," Callen confirmed, his voice steady despite what he was saying. "I'm the one tied to the runes. My blood was used during the pack binding; my blood has to be used to break it. It makes sense, I suppose – there has to be symmetry, balance."

He continued scanning the ritual instructions, his expression growing more troubled with each line. Suddenly, he went very still. Toni watched as all the colour drained from his face.

"What?" she asked, her heart rate picking up. "What else?"

"The location," he said, his voice shaking. "The ritual has to be performed in the exact spot where the binding was originally created." He looked up at her, amber eyes wide with something that looked unsettlingly like fear. "We have to go back to the pack's hideout."

Toni felt her stomach drop. They'd barely made it out of there alive when they'd stolen the box. Going back would be suicide. "But…"

"That's where Rogan bound me to the pack." Callen's voice was bitter. "Of course it would have to be there. The magic demands symmetry, remember?"

Toni began pacing the small confines of the kitchen area with renewed vigour. "This is completely insane. We're not wizards or shamans or whatever the hell kind of people usually do this sort of thing. And now we have to perform this ritual right under Rogan's nose? After what we just pulled? The pack will want us dead now!"

"Toni." Callen's voice cut through her spiral of panic, steady and firm but somehow gentle at the same time. "If we don't do this, there's no coming back for me. I'm not asking you to like it – hell, I don't like it – but I am asking for your help. Going back there…" He swallowed hard. "Trust me, it's the last thing

I want to do. But I can't do this alone, and you're the only person I trust to try."

Toni stopped pacing and leaned against the counter, studying him. "Ok. If we're doing this – and I can't believe I'm saying this – we're doing it my way. No rushing in without thoroughly checking everything, no unnecessary risks, no heroic last-minute changes to the plan. We follow the instructions exactly, we plan for every contingency, and we figure out how to secure that room long enough to complete the ritual."

"The pack will smell us the moment we enter their territory," Callen warned.

"Then we need a way to mask our scents. Or better yet, a distraction." She started writing rapidly. "Something to draw them away from that section of the building. How long will the ritual take?"

Callen consulted the papers again. "Twenty minutes, minimum. Possibly longer if anything goes wrong."

"So we plan for thirty." She paused. "What about the maintenance tunnels under the complex? You mentioned them when we were planning to steal the box."

"They're partially flooded this time of year, but they might work as an entry point. The water would help mask our scents, at least initially," he offered. "We'd need to time it perfectly with the moonrise though. The ritual is specific about that."

"Of course it is," Toni muttered. "And we'll need those other supplies – salt, iron..." She glanced at him. "How much blood are we talking about here?"

Callen's expression tightened. "More than I'd like."

"That's not reassuring."

"None of this is reassuring," he pointed out. "But it's better than the alternative."

Toni sighed heavily, running her fingers through her hair. The magnitude of what they were planning pressed down on her. They weren't just sneaking into hostile territory – they were planning to perform dangerous blood magic in the heart of a wolf shifter den led by an alpha with a grudge to settle.

"Tell me every detail about the building's layout, every security measure Rogan put in place. We're not walking into this blind."

The next few hours passed in a blur of preparation and increasingly specific instructions. Floor plans were drawn and redrawn, timing was calculated down to the minute, and backup plans were created for their backup plans. By the time the sun began to rise, casting long shadows across Toni's coffee table, they had the bones of a strategy that might – *might* – not get them killed.

"We're done for tonight," Toni insisted, seeing the exhaustion etched in Callen's features. "Go out and get the supplies we need, and take my keys with you. I might be asleep by the time you get back. We both need to rest if we're going to pull this off."

As she watched him gather his things to leave, Toni couldn't shake the feeling that they were planning either something brilliantly brave or monumentally stupid.

Possibly both. But looking at the box on her coffee table, its runes still writhing with that unsettling energy, she knew they didn't have a choice.

Chapter Eight

When Toni finally opened her eyes, the quality of light filtering through her threadbare curtains told her something was off. She fumbled for her phone, squinting at the screen: 5:47pm. She'd slept the entire day away.

Rolling onto her back, she let out a long breath. Maybe it was for the best – they'd need all their energy for tonight. The thought sent a flutter of anxiety through her stomach, but she pushed it down. No shift at Pizza Time to worry about, at least.

The ceiling above her bed had a crack that reminded her of a lightning bolt. As she traced it with her eyes, the sheer absurdity of her situation hit her. Less than a week ago, her biggest concerns had been dealing with drunk customers trying to order extra toppings at 2am and figuring out how to get her broken-down motorbike fixed. Now here she was, an ordinary human preparing to perform some ancient blood ritual in a wolf shifter den. The bike was probably still there, gathering rust under that flickering streetlight, looking just as abandoned as it had the night it had given up on her.

The smell of frying bacon drifted under her door, and her stomach growled in response. As she padded out of her bedroom, still in yesterday's clothes, the sight that greeted her brought a tired smile to her face. There was Callen, working her ancient stovetop like a professional chef, a full English breakfast coming together under his careful attention.

"You didn't have to," she said, though they both knew it was just a formality at this point. This was his way – making her breakfast for dinner, a means of saying thank you when words felt inadequate.

The bacon sizzled as Callen slid it onto her plate, alongside eggs that were perfectly done – just runny enough without being undercooked. Toni noticed his own plate was piled significantly higher. "Need to keep my strength up," he explained, catching her glance. "Blood magic takes a toll."

She picked up her fork, trying not to think too hard about that last part. "Did you get everything?"

Callen nodded towards the living area, where several bags sat clustered around the runed box. "Iron filings from a DIY supply shop. Rock salt – had to visit three different places to get enough." He pulled out a small velvet bag that clinked softly. "And some other supplies that might help."

Toni pushed her eggs around the plate, gathering her courage. "Tell me more about the pack. About Rogan. I think I need to understand more about what we're walking into."

Callen's jaw tightened, but after a moment he nodded. "Rogan... he rules through fear. Makes everyone dependent on him, convinces them they're nothing without the pack – without him. He takes in wolf shifters who are lost, vulnerable, and instead of helping them grow stronger, he breaks them down until they can't imagine surviving on their own."

"Like a cult leader," Toni said quietly.

"Exactly like that. He..." Callen's hands clenched on the table. "He'd make examples of anyone who questioned him. Force them to submit in front of everyone, sometimes make them stay in wolf form for days – without food – until they were so exhausted they'd agree to anything. And the worse part was, most of the pack convinced themselves it was normal. That it was for their own good."

"But you didn't."

A bitter smile crossed his face. "No. I saw what he was doing. How he'd pit pack members against each other, spread rumours, keep everyone off balance. Classic abuser tactics. When I tried to help others see it..." He shook his head. "That's when the tension really started between us. When it reached the point of no return, when Rogan began to see me as a threat to his authority, I knew I couldn't stay with the pack. I had to leave for my own sanity, and probably safety too."

"I guess even though pack life can be brutal and cruel, most wolf shifters must gravitate towards it because it's all they've ever known."

"That's right," he replied, a flicker of regret crossing his features. "As wolf shifters, it's in our nature to run with a pack. When I made it clear that I was going to leave, you could have cut the air with a knife. Not only is it frowned upon to leave your pack, but unusual too – it goes against everything that wolves were born to do. As you can imagine, the taboo of it can cause shame and embarrassment to an alpha – especially one like Rogan who's insecure and doesn't have the qualities of a true leader."

They ate in silence after that, both lost in their own thoughts. Toni found herself studying Callen's face, thinking about everything he must have endured. The thought made her stomach clench, but she forced herself to finish eating. They'd need the energy.

As the sky outside deepened to purple, they began their preparations. Toni dressed in dark clothes that wouldn't restrict her movement, strapping her knife to her belt and adding a few other choice items she hoped she wouldn't need. Callen helped her load the ritual components into her backpack, each item carefully wrapped to prevent noise. The box containing his spirit anchor went in last, wrapped in layers of cloth to muffle its magical resonance.

"The moon rises at 11:42pm," he said. "We need to be in position by then." His voice was steady, but she could see the tension in his shoulders. "The blood part of the ritual... it's not going to be pleasant. I'm going to give as much blood as I possibly can – we won't get a second chance at this."

"How much are we talking?"

"Enough that I'll need time to recover afterwards. Which means if anything goes wrong..."

"Nothing's going to go wrong," Toni said firmly, not quite believing her own words.

They left her apartment building with a feeling of finality looming over them, sticking to the shadows as they made their way towards the industrial district. The city felt different tonight – more alive with hidden dangers, as if it knew what they were planning. Every rustle made Toni's heart jump, every distant howl of a dog had her reaching for her knife. She was acutely aware of how vulnerable they were.

Callen's strong physique and fluid movements, the kind that spoke of someone who could fight and win, should have been reassuring. But she knew all too well that his strength, his abilities as a wolf shifter, could only help them somewhat. If his former pack found them, it wouldn't matter how skilled or powerful he was. They would outnumber him easily, and every one of them would be just as capable as he was – maybe even more so, given their unity and ruthlessness. The thought of Callen forced to defend them alone sent a shiver down her spine.

The maintenance tunnel entrance was exactly where Callen had said it would be, hidden behind a growth of weeds and decades of neglect. The rusty grate came away with surprising ease. "They never bothered securing it," Callen explained in a whisper. "Most wolves hate being underground. Too confined."

The tunnel was narrow and half-flooded, just as he'd warned. Cold water seeped into Toni's boots as they splashed forward, guided by the beam of a small flashlight. The air was thick with the smell of mould and decay, but underneath it was something else – something wild and dangerous that made her skin prickle.

They emerged into the basement of the warehouse through a partially collapsed wall. Above them, they could hear the sounds of the pack – footsteps, voices, the occasional scrape of claws on concrete. Callen held up a hand, listening intently.

"They're agitated," he whispered. "They know something's coming."

"Good thing we brought a distraction then," Toni muttered, pulling out one of the packages from her bag. It wasn't anything fancy – just a makeshift bundle she'd put together with a little research and a lot of hope.

They moved quietly through the shadows, Callen guiding them through the labyrinth of old machinery and storage rooms. The ritual chamber was on the ground floor, but they had to set their trap first. At carefully chosen spots, they placed small bundles – pouches of wolfsbane, silver powder, and other substances she'd read about, each one designed to disrupt the enhanced senses of wolf shifters.

It wasn't exactly sophisticated, but it was something. The timing had to be perfect. At exactly 11:30pm, Toni pressed a makeshift switch – a simple timer attached to a small fan, something she'd cobbled together in a rush. The fan wouldn't blow anything impressive, but it would stir up enough of the irritants to get the pack's attention.

Almost immediately, chaos broke out above them. She heard coughing and sneezing – too much for their heightened senses to handle. The distraction was working. It wasn't elegant, but it was enough.

"Now," Callen whispered, and they moved.

They reached the ritual chamber just as the moonlight began to stream through the high windows. The runes on the floor seemed to pulse with an inner light, responding to the presence of the spirit anchor within its box. Toni felt a cold sweat forming as she looked around – this was nothing like anything she'd ever done before. As a human with no experience in magic, she'd never been part of a ritual like this. But she'd studied and listened closely, making sure she understood every step she'd need to take.

Her hands shook slightly as she began laying out the components. It wasn't graceful – she fumbled a little with the packages and jars – but she didn't let herself hesitate. She had to move quickly, but also carefully, like she was following an invisible blueprint in her mind.

Meanwhile, Callen moved with the assured precision of someone who knew this world intimately, drawing the necessary circles with iron filings and salt. Toni focused on her task, aware that every moment, every choice, had to be right. There was no room for mistakes.

The sounds of confusion in the distant background were changing to anger as the pack realised they'd been tricked. They didn't have much time.

Callen placed the runed box in the centre of the circle and began chanting – words in a language Toni didn't recognise. The runes on both the box and floor began to glow brighter, matching the rhythm of his words. She watched as he drew a deep knife slash across his palm, then his forearm, letting the blood flow freely onto the box's surface. His face was already growing pale, but his voice remained steady as he continued the chant.

The door burst open. Rogan stood in the doorway, his massive human form filling the frame, eyes blazing with fury. Behind him, the rest of the pack crouched in their wolf forms, low growls vibrating in their throats, muscles coiled and ready to spring. Their glowing eyes never left Toni and Callen, each one poised to defend their leader at a moment's notice. The only thing keeping them at bay was the line of rock salt Toni had managed to lay across the threshold, a barrier that burned with a faint but unsettling glow.

"You dare?" Rogan's voice was more growl than speech. "You think you can just walk in here and break what's mine? That bond is sacred. You have no right to sever it."

"I was never yours," Callen said, his voice steady despite the blood still flowing from his wounds. "And after tonight, I never will be."

Rogan hurled himself forward, but crashed into an invisible barrier. The combination of rock salt and the ritual's growing power had created a shield neither he nor his pack could cross. Undeterred, Rogan began his own chant, trying to interfere with the ritual.

The air grew thick with competing magic. Toni could feel it pressing against her skin like static electricity. The runes on both the box and the floor were writhing now, trying to maintain their hold on Callen even as his blood worked to dissolve the connection.

Callen's voice was growing weaker, the blood loss and magical effort taking their toll. Without thinking, Toni stepped forward and gripped his free hand. She wasn't magical, wasn't a shifter, but she could give him this – her strength, her support, her absolute conviction that he deserved to be free.

Something shifted in the air, the atmosphere suddenly thick with a charged energy that made Toni's skin prickle. The runes on the box flared blindingly bright, casting jagged shadows across the room before they began to crack like glass. The sound was deafening as the runes splintered apart, sending violent waves of light rippling outward. The box split open with a thunderous crash, revealing the bear's tooth necklace – Callen's spirit anchor, the precious token of his mother's love, now free from Rogan's suffocating control.

Toni's breath caught in her throat as Callen staggered back, his eyes wide, as if the very force of the release had knocked the air from his lungs. She could see him fighting for control as a wave of energy surged through him, his chest rising and falling with ragged breaths. Then, his posture shifted, his stance no longer burdened by the weight of the bond that had enslaved him. He was free.

But it wasn't just Callen who was affected.

Rogan, standing like a mountain of fury at the edge of the ritual chamber, howled in agony. His expression twisted with pain, his hands grasping at the air as if trying to hold on to the magic that had kept Callen tied to the pack.

The room seemed to hold its breath as the magic unravelled completely. Toni's eyes flicked to the pack members who had remained behind Rogan, their snarls and growls fading into uneasy silence. The shift in the air, the sight of their leader crumbling, was too much to ignore. The very foundation of Rogan's authority was splintering in front of them. They could feel it, even if they couldn't fully understand it. And that doubt, that crack in Rogan's power, was enough.

Toni could see it in their eyes, the flicker of hesitation. Rogan's command, his dominance – it was no longer unchallenged. The pack would no longer follow without question. The air hummed with the scent of change, and as Callen stood straighter, his body freer than it had been in years, it was clear: the pack's loyalty to Rogan was weakening. His reign had just been destabilised in the most visceral way possible.

The wolves drew back, confused and disorientated as their alpha's influence wavered. Some began to shift back to human form, looking around as if waking from a long dream.

Callen's eyes glowed not just amber now, but with an inner fire that spoke of power fully restored. He stepped forward, crossing the broken line of rock salt, and faced his former alpha. Despite the blood still seeping from his wounds, he stood tall.

"Leave," he said, his voice carrying a weight of authority that made several of the pack members whimper. "Find another territory. This one isn't yours anymore."

Rogan looked around wildly, seeing the faces of the pack members – seeing the way they now looked at Callen, some with something like hope in their eyes. His control was broken, and he knew it. With a snarl of pure hatred, he turned and fled, disappearing into the shadows of the warehouse.

A few of Rogan's most loyal followers hesitated for only a moment before running after him, fleeing into the darkness. But most of the pack remained, their eyes fixed expectantly on Callen.

"You don't have to follow him anymore," Callen said, his gaze sweeping across the pack. "Rogan's gone, and with him, his reign of terror. No more fear, no more intimidation." He paused, giving them a moment to process. "You have a choice. You can stay, help me rebuild, and we can make something better – something we choose. Or, you can go your own way, free of any binding."

A tense silence filled the air as the pack exchanged wary glances. Some of them looked to the shadows where Rogan had disappeared, as though expecting him to reappear at any moment. Others, however, seemed to shift uneasily on their feet, the gravity of Callen's words settling in.

Slowly, one by one, more of the pack members took a step forward, moving towards Callen. His shoulders relaxed slightly as he watched them gather, and he nodded in return, grateful, but determined.

"This is just the beginning," he said. "We do this together, or we don't do it at all. But I won't force anyone to stay. The choice is yours."

Satisfied that the tension in the air had eased, Toni sat down on a nearby crate, the events of the night finally catching up with her. Her hands were shaking, and every muscle ached, but they'd done it. While Callen was distracted with the pack, she noticed him hesitating to approach the broken box where the bear's tooth necklace lay. Understanding his fear, she quietly retrieved it herself, slipping it into her pocket.

Callen finished speaking with the pack and came to sit beside her. He looked exhausted but lighter somehow, as if a great burden had been lifted from him. The wounds on his arm and palm were already beginning to heal, though he'd lost enough blood to make his face ashen.

"So," she said. "What now?"

He smiled – a real smile, not the guarded one she'd grown used to seeing. "Now? Now we figure out what freedom really means." He looked around the chamber, at the scattered salt and iron filings, at the destroyed box. "But first, I think I owe you another breakfast."

Together, they walked out of the warehouse into the moonlit night. The bear's tooth necklace remained safely hidden in Toni's pocket, waiting to be returned to its rightful owner.

Chapter Nine

When Toni woke the next day, sunlight was already streaming through her threadbare curtains. For a moment, she lay there trying to piece together if the events of the previous night had been real – the ritual, the confrontation with Rogan, the shattering of the runed box. Her aching muscles and the faint traces of salt still clinging to her clothes confirmed it hadn't been a dream.

She fumbled for her phone, squinting at the screen: 12:17pm. Just enough time to get ready for her shift at Pizza Time. The thought of returning to such mundane normalcy after everything that had happened was almost comical, but there was something oddly comforting about it too. Even after helping to break a magical pack bond and confronting a tyrannical alpha, bills still needed to be paid.

In the bathroom, Toni scrubbed at her arms and hands, making sure there were no traces of dried blood from Callen's part in the ritual. "Can't exactly show up to work with wolf shifter blood on me," she muttered to herself with a wry smile. "They might have something to say about that."

When she emerged from the bathroom, she found Callen sprawled across her worn couch, dead to the world. He'd stripped off his shirt in his sleep, probably overheated from the residual energy of the ritual. Toni found herself drawn closer, eyes tracing over his chest where intricate tattoos marked his skin. But the runes that had once lurked beneath them, the magical bonds that had tied him to Rogan's pack, were gone. The sight made her heart lighter – tangible proof that they'd succeeded, that he was truly free.

She thought about waking him, but decided against it. After everything – the blood loss, the magical exertion, the emotional toll – he needed the rest. Something tugged at her instincts then, and she found herself stepping back into her bedroom. The bear's tooth necklace was right where she'd left it on her bedside table, and though she couldn't explain why, something in her gut told her she needed to keep it close. She slipped it into her pocket before gathering her things and sneaking quietly out of the apartment, trying not to think too hard about whether he'd still be there when she returned.

The bus ride to work gave her time to think. Her motorbike was still abandoned under that flickering streetlight near Pizza Time, assuming no one had stolen or vandalised it yet. Either way, she'd have to walk the three miles home after her shift.

The familiar rhythm of her shift provided an almost surreal contrast to the previous night's events. As she prepared pizzas, took orders, and dealt with the usual array of customers who couldn't remember which drink they'd ordered, her mind kept drifting back to the warehouse. The way Callen had stood up to Rogan, the power in his voice when he'd addressed the pack, the hope in the eyes of those who'd chosen to stay.

She found herself wondering about pack life, realising how little she really knew about that world despite everything she'd learnt from Callen. The thought made her smile – maybe she should make a habit of taking in stray wolves. Though she doubted any future encounters would be quite as eventful as this one had been.

"You're in a good mood today," one of her colleagues commented as she cleared the worktop, his thick-framed glasses slipping down his nose as he absentmindedly wiped his flour-dusted hands on his apron.

"Just one of those days," she replied, unable to explain that she was thinking about how she'd helped overthrow a dictatorial alpha wolf the night before.

As her shift wound down, she went through the closing routine on autopilot – wiping down tables, restocking condiments, closing the till. Greg, her perpetually aloof boss, barely looked up from his phone as she called out her goodbye.

The night air was cool as she started her walk home, deciding to take the route past her abandoned bike. She needed to know if it was still there, even if there wasn't much she could do about it either way. The familiar flickering streetlight came into view, and she felt a surge of relief at seeing the bike still parked beneath it, apparently untouched.

"Checking up on your ride?"

Toni spun around, startled, to find Callen standing behind her. There was something different about him now – a lightness to his movements, an ease in his stance that she hadn't seen before. Freedom looked good on him.

"I wasn't expecting to see you," she said, pleased that he looked so well.

His smile was warm. "I wanted to surprise you. I had the bike fixed."

"You what?"

"It was the least I could do after everything you've done for me. You gave me a place to stay, took a chance on a stranger, made my problems your own. I don't take that lightly."

Toni ran a hand along the bike's frame, happily noticing that it had also been cleaned. "It was actually kind of nice, you know? A break from my boring life."

"About that..." Callen's expression turned serious, though his eyes remained kind. "You've got skills, Toni. The research you did, the way you helped me get my head around so many of the challenges – that's not something just anyone could have done, especially someone with no previous knowledge of my world. And the courage it took to stand beside me in that warehouse?" He shook his head in admiration. "You're capable of so much more than serving pizzas and struggling to get by."

The words hit home in a way Toni hadn't expected, stirring something that had been dormant for a long time. Maybe he was right. Maybe there were other paths she could explore, other ways to use the abilities she'd discovered in herself.

"I'm going to focus on the pack now," Callen continued. "They need leadership – real leadership, not what Rogan gave them. It's time for me to step up, to be the alpha they deserve instead of the omega I was forced to be." He must have seen the flicker of sadness cross her face, because he quickly added, "You're welcome on pack territory anytime.

That's not an invitation we extend to many humans."

"I appreciate that," Toni said softly. Then, sensing he would want to return to his pack soon, she reached into her pocket. "I should give you this." She pulled out the bear's tooth necklace, holding it out almost apologetically, knowing it might carry painful memories after how Rogan had used it against him.

Callen's breath caught as he saw what she was holding. His fingers trembled slightly as he reached for it, and though he didn't cry, his eyes grew bright with unshed tears. "You grabbed it," he said, his voice thick with emotion. "You thought to save it."

"I knew how much it meant to you," Toni said quietly.

Callen clutched the necklace tightly, his knuckles white. "This stays with me forever now," he declared, his voice certain despite its tremor. "Never again will I hand it over to any alpha, no matter what ritual or ceremony they claim requires it. No more bullies using it to control me."

A warmth spread through Toni's chest, a quiet pride swelling inside her.

"And hey," Callen added with a gentle smile, recovering his composure, "maybe someday you'll get a dog. You've got good instincts – knew exactly what to do with a stray wolf in his hour of need. You're a good person, Toni. Even when you're bored and pissed off at the world, there's something special about you. What you did for me proves that. The future's bright for you, if you want it to be."

Before she could respond, he turned and walked away, disappearing into the shadows between streetlights. She watched until she couldn't see him anymore, then turned back to her bike. The engine started on the first try, purring like it was brand new.

As she rode home through the quiet streets, she felt something unfamiliar building inside – not just hope, but possibility. The world was bigger than she'd imagined, full of chances to be more than she'd dared to believe. Maybe it was time to find out just how far she could go.

After all, she'd already helped overthrow one tyrannical wolf shifter. What else might she be capable of?

The city stretched out before her, a maze of streetlights and shadows, ordinary and extraordinary all at once. Somewhere out there, a pack of wolf shifters was beginning to heal, led by someone who understood both strength and kindness. Somewhere out there, magic thrummed beneath the surface of the everyday world, waiting to be discovered by those who dared to look deeper.

And somewhere out there, her own path was waiting – one that led far beyond the walls of Pizza Time and the confines of what she'd thought possible. She wasn't sure exactly where that path would take her, but for the first time in years, she was ready to find out.

Toni smiled, revved her engine, and rode into the night. The moon hung full and bright above her, promising adventures yet to come.